THE ROSE IN MY GARDEN

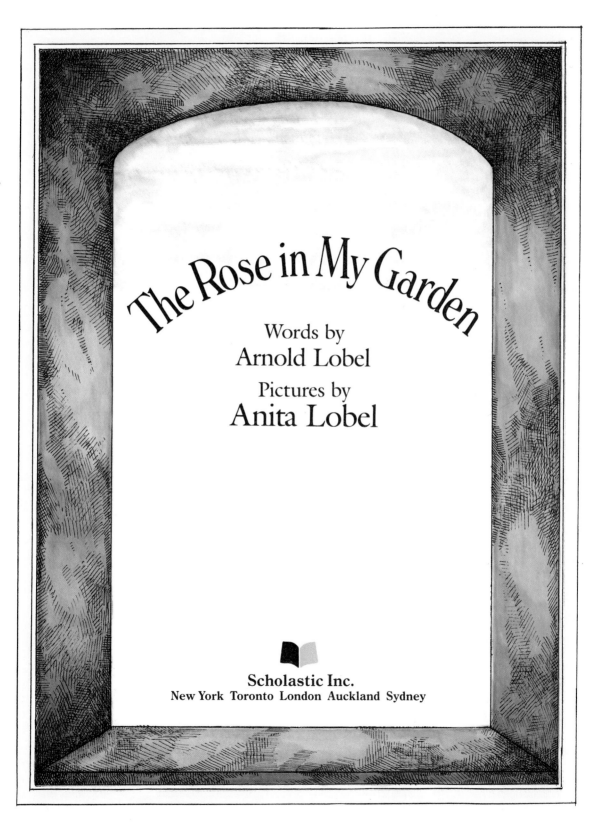

The Rose in My Garden

Words by
Arnold Lobel

Pictures by
Anita Lobel

Scholastic Inc.
New York Toronto London Auckland Sydney

ISBN 0-590-41530-1

12 11 10 9 8 7 6   1 2/9

Printed in the U.S.A.   08

FOR
WILLIAM GRAY

AND
JAMES MARSHALL

This is the rose in my garden.

This is the bee
That sleeps on the rose in my garden.

These are the hollyhocks high above ground,
That give shade to the bee
That sleeps on the rose in my garden.

These are the marigolds orange and round,
That stand by the hollyhocks high above ground,
That give shade to the bee
That sleeps on the rose in my garden.

These are the zinnias straight in a row,
That grow near the marigolds orange and round,
That stand by the hollyhocks high above ground.
That give shade to the bee
That sleeps on the rose in my garden.

These are the daisies as white as the snow,
That border the zinnias straight in a row,
That grow near the marigolds orange and round,
That stand by the hollyhocks high above ground,
That give shade to the bee
That sleeps on the rose in my garden.

These are the bluebells with petals like lace,
That shelter the daisies as white as the snow,
That border the zinnias straight in a row,
That grow near the marigolds orange and round,
That stand by the hollyhocks high above ground,
That give shade to the bee
That sleeps on the rose in my garden.

These are the lilies of elegant grace,
That lean toward the bluebells with petals like lace,
That shelter the daisies as white as the snow,
That border the zinnias straight in a row,
That grow near the marigolds orange and round,
That stand by the hollyhocks high above ground,
That give shade to the bee
That sleeps on the rose in my garden.

These are the peonies pleasingly plump,
That are close to the lilies of elegant grace,
That lean toward the bluebells with petals like lace,
That shelter the daisies as white as the snow,
That border the zinnias straight in a row,
That grow near the marigolds orange and round,
That stand by the hollyhocks high above ground,
That give shade to the bee
That sleeps on the rose in my garden.

These are the pansies placed in a clump,
That crowd all the peonies pleasingly plump,
That are close to the lilies of elegant grace,
That lean toward the bluebells with petals like lace,
That shelter the daisies as white as the snow,
That border the zinnias straight in a row,
That grow near the marigolds orange and round,
That stand by the hollyhocks high above ground,
That give shade to the bee
That sleeps on the rose in my garden.

These are the tulips sturdy and tall,
That circle the pansies placed in a clump,
That crowd all the peonies pleasingly plump,
That are close to the lilies of elegant grace,
That lean toward the bluebells with petals like lace,
That shelter the daisies as white as the snow,
That border the zinnias straight in a row,
That grow near the marigolds orange and round,
That stand by the hollyhocks high above ground,
That give shade to the bee
That sleeps on the rose in my garden.

These are the sunflowers tallest of all,
That rise by the tulips sturdy and tall,
That circle the pansies placed in a clump,
That crowd all the peonies pleasingly plump,
That are close to the lilies of elegant grace,
That lean toward the bluebells with petals like lace,
That shelter the daisies as white as the snow,
That border the zinnias straight in a row,
That grow near the marigolds orange and round,
That stand by the hollyhocks high above ground,
That give shade to the bee
That sleeps on the rose in my garden.

This is the fieldmouse shaking in fear,
That hides by the sunflowers tallest of all,
That rise by the tulips sturdy and tall,
That circle the pansies placed in a clump,
That crowd all the peonies pleasingly plump,
That are close to the lilies of elegant grace,
That lean toward the bluebells with petals like lace,
That shelter the daisies as white as the snow,
That border the zinnias straight in a row,
That grow near the marigolds orange and round,
That stand by the hollyhocks high above ground,
That give shade to the bee
That sleeps on the rose in my garden.

This is the cat with the tattered ear,
That chases the fieldmouse shaking in fear,

That shudders the sunflowers tallest of all,
That shivers the tulips sturdy and tall,
That quivers the pansies placed in a clump,
That pushes the peonies pleasingly plump,
That startles the lilies of elegant grace,
That shatters the bluebells with petals like lace,

That scatters the daisies as white as the snow,
That rattles the zinnias straight in a row,
That mangles the marigolds orange and round,
That tangles the hollyhocks high above ground,
That give shade to the bee…

THAT WAKES UP ON THE ROSE IN MY GARDEN!

This is the rose in my garden.

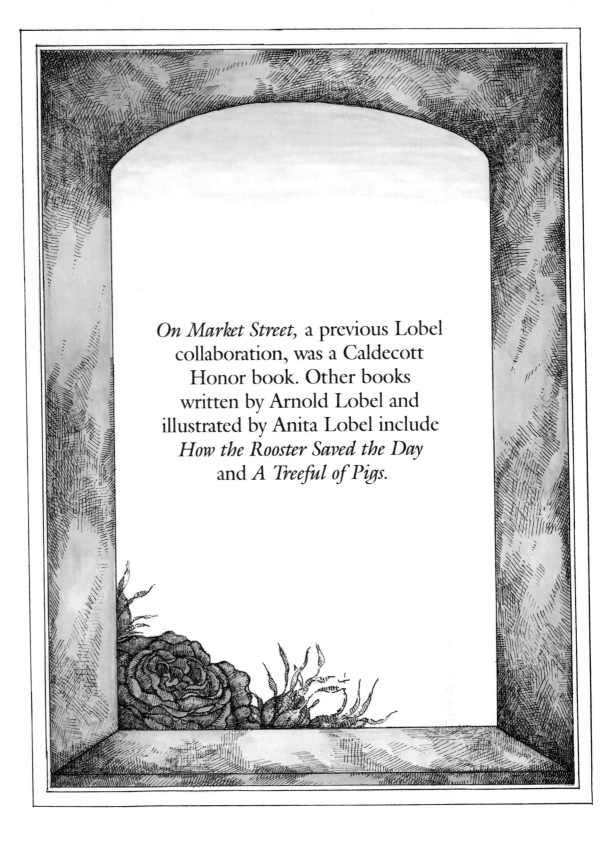

On Market Street, a previous Lobel
collaboration, was a Caldecott
Honor book. Other books
written by Arnold Lobel and
illustrated by Anita Lobel include
How the Rooster Saved the Day
and *A Treeful of Pigs.*